WELCOME TO
PASSPORT TO READING
A beginning reader's ticket to a brand-new world!

Every book in this program is designed to build read-along and read-alone skills, level by level, through engaging and enriching stories. As the reader turns each page, he or she will become more confident with new vocabulary, sight words, and comprehension.

These PASSPORT TO READING levels will help you choose the perfect book for every reader.

 READING TOGETHER
Read short words in simple sentence structures together to begin a reader's journey.

 READING OUT LOUD
Encourage developing readers to sound out words in more complex stories with simple vocabulary.

 READING INDEPENDENTLY
Newly independent readers gain confidence reading more complex sentences with higher word counts.

 READY TO READ MORE
Readers prepare for chapter books with fewer illustrations and longer paragraphs.

This book features sight words from the educator-supported Dolch Sight Words List. This encourages the reader to recognize commonly used vocabulary words, increasing reading speed and fluency.

For more information, please visit passporttoreadingbooks.com.

Enjoy the journey!

marvelkids.com

© 2016 MARVEL

Little, Brown and Company
Hachette Book Group
1290 Avenue of the Americas, New York, NY 10104

Visit us at lb-kids.com

Little, Brown and Company is a division of Hachette Book Group, Inc.
The Little, Brown name and logo are trademarks of Hachette Book Group, Inc.

The publisher is not responsible for websites (or their content) that are not owned by the publisher.

First Edition: April 2016

Library of Congress Control Number: 2016932125

ISBN 978-0-316-27144-8

10 9 8 7 6 5 4 3 2 1

CW

Printed in the United States of America

Passport to Reading titles are leveled by independent reviewers applying the standards developed by Irene Fountas and Gay Su Pinnell in *Matching Books to Readers: Using Leveled Books in Guided Reading*, Heinemann, 1999.

MARVEL

CIVIL WAR

CAPTAIN AMERICA

ESCAPE FROM BLACK PANTHER

Adapted by R. R. Busse

Illustrated by Ron Lim, Andy Smith, and Andy Troy

Based on the screenplay by Christopher Markus
and Stephen McFeely

Produced by Kevin Feige

Directed by Anthony and Joe Russo

Ⓛ Ⓑ

LITTLE, BROWN AND COMPANY
New York   Boston

Attention, Captain America fans!
Look for these words
when you read this book.
Can you spot them all?

explosion

shield

claws

armor

This is Captain America.

His real name is Steve Rogers.

He is very brave.

He sees an explosion.

Cap knows people will blame
his friend Bucky Barnes
for the explosion.
Bucky used to do bad things
as the Winter Soldier.

Cap races to Bucky.

His home looks empty.

Just then the police
arrive to fight.
Bucky grabs Cap's shield.
He saves them both!

Then, he runs away.

Bucky jumps from roof to roof to escape.

Bucky does not see
the stranger chasing him.
Captain America does.

It is Black Panther!

He has sharp claws and is really strong.

Black Panther's claws hit
Bucky's metal arm.
Captain America uses
his shield for cover.

Black Panther does not need a shield.
Nothing hurts him.

Bucky jumps off the roof.

Black Panther follows him.

He uses his claws on the wall!

Bucky takes a motorcycle.

He needs to get out of there!

Black Panther is not far behind.

Black Panther and Bucky fight on the motorcycle.
Bucky almost loses control!

Bucky throws out a silver ball.
It is a distraction!

Black Panther does not give up.

He attacks Bucky again.

Black Panther is winning the fight!

Captain America runs
to help his friend.
Black Panther claws his shield.

Captain America's shield is very strong.
Black Panther's claws are too sharp.
They scratch the shield!

Blasts come from the sky!

It is Iron Man's friend Rhodey.

He has his own suit of armor.

He is called War Machine.

War Machine helps the police arrest Bucky.

Bucky is surrounded.

How will Captain America save his friend?